Dear Parent:

Parents cut star- and flower-shaped vegetables, make clown face salads, construct racing cars made out of celery, carrots, and peanut butter—all to get children to eat nutritious food!

Dinner at the Panda Palace is the perfect solution for these anxious parents. Never before has eating been so much fun! Just look at the hilarious details in the illustrations: crocodile waiters, monkeys swinging from chandeliers, peacocks, pigs, and Mr. Panda himself.

What's more, this is a counting book. Teachers now say that picture books can help instill math concepts in a way that academic exercises cannot. Not only is reading Dinner at the Panda Palace enjoyable—your child will learn to count to ten, also. (For advanced counters, there are fifty-six visitors in all to the Panda Palace.)

So, turn the page and let the Panda Palace serve up some fun!

Sincerely,

Stephen Fraser

Stephen Fraser
Senior Editor
Weekly Reader Books

Weekly Reader Children's Book Club Presents

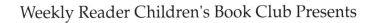

Dinner at the Panda Palace

by Stephanie Calmenson

illustrated by Nadine Bernard Westcott

HarperCollins*Publishers*

To Anna Smeragliuolo
—S.C.

For Wendy
—N.W.

This book is a presentation of Newfield Publications, Inc.
Newfield Publications offers book clubs for children
from preschool through high school. For further
information write to: **Newfield Publications, Inc.,**
4343 Equity Drive, Columbus, Ohio 43228.

Published by arrangement with HarperCollins Publishers.
Newfield Publications is a trademark
of Newfield Publications, Inc.
Weekly Reader is a federally registered trademark
of Weekly Reader Corporation.

DINNER AT THE PANDA PALACE

Text copyright © 1991 by Stephanie Calmenson
Illustrations copyright © 1991 by Nadine Bernard Westcott
Printed in the U.S.A. All rights reserved.
Typography by Elynn Cohen

1 2 3 4 5 6 7 8 9 10
First Edition

Library of Congress Cataloging-in-Publication Data
Calmenson, Stephanie.
    Dinner at the Panda Palace / by Stephanie Calmanson ; illustrated
by Nadine Bernard Westcott.
        p.   cm.
    Summary: Mr. Panda, owner of the Panda Palace restaurant, manages
to find seating for all of his animal patrons on a very busy night.
    ISBN 0-06-021010-9. — ISBN 0-06-021011-7 (lib. bdg.)
    [1. Restaurants, lunch rooms, etc.—Fiction. 2. Pandas—Fiction.
3. Animals—Fiction. 4. Stories in rhyme.] I. Westcott, Nadine
Bernard, ill. II Title.
PZ8.C13DI   1991   90-33720
[E]—dc20   CIP
                                                                            AC

The Panda Palace opened

At six one night.

All the tables were ready.

The room was just right.

As the diners arrived,

They were graciously greeted.

Mr. Panda himself

Helped each one get seated.

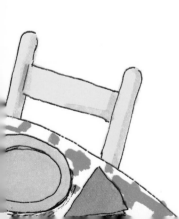

An elephant came first
With a trunk that was gray.
He'd been out on the road
Selling peanuts all day.

"I'm enormously hungry.
My bag weighs a ton.
I would like to sit down.
Have you a table for one?"

The lions came next.

They were dropped off outside.

"Welcome, Your Highnesses.

How was your ride?"

"Traffic was awful.

The bumps were bad, too.

We are so glad to be here.

Is there a table for two?"

Along came some pigs,

Who needed to hide.

"Quick, Mr. Panda.

Let us inside!

"There's a wolf on our trail.

We must lose him, you see.

We'll stay here for dinner.

Have you a table for three?"

A proud group of peacocks,

With feathers fanned wide,

Was a most splendid sight

For the others inside.

With heads held up high

They walked through the door.

"Do we need reservations?

Or can you seat four?"

And then, one by one,

The monkeys arrived.

They went swinging across

To their table for five.

The giraffes had just painted

The rooftops in town.

"If there's a table for six,

We would like to sit down."

The hyenas walked in

And laughed right out loud.

They never had seen

Such a wonderful crowd!

"We've come from afar

For our family meeting.

There are seven of us.

We do hope you have seating."

A party of penguins

Coming straight from a ball

Waddled in through the door,

Hats, jewels and all.

"This is just the right place

For our elegant date.

Please, Mr. Panda,

Is there a table for eight?"

The Honey Bear All-Stars,

With gloves, balls, and bats,

Had played a great game

With the Tiger-Striped Cats.

"We hit three home runs,
So we're feeling just fine.
Now it's time for a party.
Is there room here for nine?"

Here a chick, there a chick.

Where's mother hen?

Oh, here she comes now

To her table for ten.

The restaurant was humming.

The waiters moved fast.

Feeding fifty-five diners

Was no easy task.

Then through all the noise

Came a knock at the door.

A tiny mouse asked,

"Is there room for one more?"

Mr. Panda looked left.

Mr. Panda looked right.

All the tables were filled

At the Palace that night.

Did he say, "I am sorry,

We have a full house;

We can't fit one more,

Not even a mouse"?

No! Not Mr. Panda!

He found one more seat.

In no time the mouse

Had a fine meal to eat.

So if ever you're hungry

And going that way,

Just see Mr. Panda.

Here's what he'll say:

"No matter how many,

No matter how few,

There will always be room

At the Palace for you!"